Puffin Books

MR MAJEIKA AND THE DINNER LADY

The members of Class Three know all about the magical powers of their wizard teacher, Mr Majeika. But they still come in for a few surprises, especially when things don't work out quite as he intends. Always eager to help his pupils out of a tight spot, Mr Majeika's eccentric behaviour sometimes threatens to make situations worse rather than better. Take his personal recipe for toad-in-the-hole, for example...

But his spells have a way of working out in the end, and grumpy Mrs Chipchase and nasty Wilhelmina Worlock are put in their places. Even the class nuisance, Hamish Bigmore, gets his come-uppance – but not until he's caused as much chaos as he can.

In this latest collection of stories, Mr Majeika and his exploits are as unexpected and full of fun as ever.

Humphrey Carpenter is well known as a writer and has published biographies of Tolkien, C.S. Lewis and the Inklings, and W.H. Auden. In 1984 his major study, *The Oxford Companion to Children's Literature*, was published to great acclaim. He is the author of several children's books, including the Mr Majeika series. He lives in Oxford with his wife and two daughters.

HUMPHREY CARPENTER

Mr Majeika
and the Dinner Lady

ILLUSTRATED BY FRANK RODGERS

PUFFIN BOOKS

PUFFIN BOOKS

Published by the Penguin Group
27 Wrights Lane, London W8 5TZ, England
Viking Penguin Inc., 40 West 23rd Street, New York, New York 10010, USA
Penguin Books Australia Ltd, Ringwood, Victoria, Australia
Penguin Books Canada Ltd, 2801 John Street, Markham, Ontario, Canada L3R 1B4
Penguin Books (NZ) Ltd, 182–190 Wairau Road, Auckland 10, New Zealand

Penguin Books Ltd, Registered Offices: Harmondsworth, Middlesex, England

First published by Viking Kestrel 1989
Published in Puffin Books 1990
10 9 8 7 6 5 4 3 2 1

Text copyright © Humphrey Carpenter, 1989
Illustrations copyright © Frank Rodgers, 1989
All rights reserved

Made and printed in Great Britain by
Cox and Wyman Ltd, Reading, Berks.
Filmset in Palatino (Linotron 202)

With thanks to Mr Fitzgerald's and Mrs-Andrews-upstairs's classes at Oxford East First School, and to two people I had better call X and Y, who told me about *their* dinner lady.

Contents

1. *Mrs Chipchase's Favourite Friend*

'I hate school dinners,' said Thomas, chewing his way through a piece of sausage. All around him, Class Three were gloomily sticking their knives and forks into platefuls of sausage, mashed potatoes and peas.

'We all hate school dinners,' said his twin brother, Peter, who was trying to

wash down his own tough leathery sausage with a glass of water.

'That's right,' said their friend, Jody. 'There's nothing special about you hating them, Thomas.'

'But I hate them more than anyone else does,' said Thomas, speaking with his mouth full, because his own bit of sausage refused to go down even though he had been chewing it for about ten minutes. 'I hate them so much I wake up in the night screaming about them.'

'He doesn't,' said Peter, 'He sleeps like a log.'

'Ah, but I have nightmares about them,' said Thomas. 'I had a nightmare the other night that I was in the factory where school dinners were being made. It was full of the slimy insides of monsters, mixed up with huge barrels of green sludge marked Poison.'

'That's right,' said Pete. 'That's what it must be like in the place where they cook them. Ugh, this sausage has got bones in it.'

'You're both being a bit silly,' said Jody. 'I know the food is awful, but it isn't *that* bad. And anyway, it's made here in the school kitchen by Cook. If you don't like it, why not complain to her?'

'Complain to Cook?' said Thomas, laughing scornfully. 'We'd never get a chance. You know who'd stop us, don't you?'

'Be quiet, you three,' snapped a voice, 'or I'll send you outside.' It was Mrs Chipchase, the dinner lady who, as usual, was very red in the face.

Mrs Chipchase had been in charge

of dinners at St Barty's School for as long as anyone could remember –

since before Mr Potter became head teacher, and long before Mr Majeika had arrived to teach Class Three. Mr Majeika was a wizard, though nobody outside Class Three knew this, and since he had arrived all sorts of exciting things had happened.

Thomas, Jody and Pete thought Mr Majeika was wonderful. In fact, all Class Three liked Mr Majeika – all except Hamish Bigmore, the class nuisance. When Mr Majeika first arrived Hamish Bigmore had refused to do what he was told, so Mr Majeika had turned him into a frog, and since then Hamish had never forgiven him. He'd tried to make life difficult for Mr Majeika at every opportunity, and there had been all sorts of strange magical occurrences as a result of Hamish's trouble-making. Mr Majeika wasn't supposed to do magic now that he had become a teacher, but sometimes he forgot this and the most peculiar things happened.

In fact, life had been really very pleasant for Class Three – except that Mrs Chipchase was their dinner lady.

She was always very bad-tempered, and she kept on sending people out for talking or for being cheeky to her, and she made them report to Mr Potter who was supposed to punish them. Mr Potter usually didn't punish them, because he could see that Mrs Chipchase was horrid to the children. But as she had been at St Barty's much longer than anyone else, he didn't like to argue with her.

'Sometimes,' whispered Jody, 'I think school dinners would be all right if it wasn't for her.'

'Yes,' answered Pete. 'The food isn't *that* revolting – it's having to watch her march up and down, ranting and raving, which makes it so awful.'

'Right, you lot!' snapped Mrs Chipchase. 'I heard that. It's off to Mr

Potter with the three of you.' And she
marched them out of the room still
shouting at them, like a dog barking at
sheep.

'Bye, bye,' said a voice from the
corner. 'Don't you wish you had a
nice yummy lunch like me?' It was
Hamish Bigmore, and as usual he was

eating a large bar of chocolate.

'That's what makes it even worse,'

Jody said to Mr Majeika after lessons that afternoon. 'We have to eat that awful food and be shouted at by Mrs Chipchase for talking, and all the time Hamish is sitting in the corner stuffing chocolate in his mouth.'

'Chocolate?' said Mr Majeika. 'But you're not allowed to bring chocolate or sweets to school. Surely Mrs Chipchase should report Hamish Bigmore to Mr Potter for that?'

'Ah,' said Pete, 'but you see, Hamish Bigmore doesn't bring the chocolate to school.'

'What do you mean?' asked Mr Majeika.

Thomas, Jody and Pete looked at each other. 'We don't like telling tales,' said Thomas. 'But you could come and see for yourself, couldn't you, Mr Majeika? Why not come and

eat school dinner with us tomorrow?'

Mr Majeika sighed. 'I do enjoy my sandwiches in the staff room,' he said sadly. 'I have a very peaceful half-hour in there. Still, if something peculiar is going on . . .'

'What d'you mean, there aren't enough knives and forks?' Mrs

Chipchase snapped at Jody. 'Trying to teach me my job, are you, after I've been at St Barty's for thirty-five years? D'you want me to send you to Mr Potter?'

'No, no, Mrs Chipchase,' said Jody hastily. 'I didn't mean to upset you. But Mr Majeika, our class teacher, is coming in to have lunch with us today.'

'Your teacher, coming to have school dinner?' Mrs Chipchase said, breathing heavily and looking more red in the face than ever. 'What's a teacher doing having school dinner? Teachers don't have school dinners. They eat their sandwiches in the staff room. I'll have a word with Mr Potter about this. Teacher, indeed!'

'Oh, please, Mrs Chipchase,' said Jody, 'he's only coming in here for the one day. And it's because he's heard how nice the food is.'

'Oh?' said Mrs Chipchase, stopping in her tracks.

'Yes,' said Thomas, 'and we've told him how clever you are at keeping order – you know, at telling everyone to be quiet and all that.'

'Oh?' said Mrs Chipchase suspiciously. 'Have you just?'

'That's right,' said Pete. 'And he says he's very interested in watching you do it, because teachers often find it very difficult to keep order, and he says he thinks he could learn a lot from you.'

'Oh?' said Mrs Chipchase. 'Does he just? Well, he'd better watch his step and behave himself, teacher or no teacher!'

Ten minutes later Mr Majeika was sitting next to Thomas, Jody and Pete, trying to struggle through the meal.

'This is awful!' he whispered. 'My fellow wizards and witches used to eat plates of juicy wriggling worms in bogweed sauce and it was quite delicious, but *this* – this looks like worms all right, but they're dead! We always ate ours alive.'

Pete burst out laughing. 'It's spaghetti in tomato sauce!'

'Be quiet over there!' snapped a voice. 'There's some people in this school as call themselves *teachers*, when to my mind they're just trouble-makers. Don't forget, anyone who makes a noise will be sent to Mr Potter – and I mean *anyone*.' Mrs Chipchase looked pointedly at Mr Majeika.

'You'd better watch out,' giggled Thomas. 'You don't want to be sent to Mr Potter, do you, Mr Majeika?'

Mr Majeika toyed mournfully with his spaghetti. 'But what about Hamish Bigmore?' he whispered.

'Can't you see?' answered Jody. 'He's not having to eat school dinner, is he?'

Hamish Bigmore certainly wasn't

having to eat school dinner. He was sitting at a separate table all by himself, and in front of him was spread a most delicious packed lunch.

'He's brought his own food,' Thomas explained.

'But why don't you all do that?' whispered Mr Majeika. 'Then you wouldn't have to eat these dead worms and all the other awful things.'

'We're not allowed to,' said Pete. 'The school rule is no packed lunches. It's a rule that was made before Mr Potter's time, and I can guess who made it.'

'Mrs Chipchase?' whispered Mr Majeika.

Thomas nodded. 'She and Cook. I bet *they* made that rule, so that everyone would have to eat Cook's dreadful food.'

'So why,' asked Mr Majeika, 'is Hamish allowed to bring a packed lunch?'

'Because he's Mrs Chipchase's favourite friend,' answered Jody. 'That's what she always calls him, "My favourite friend."'

'Why on earth?' asked Mr Majeika, shuddering.

'Well,' whispered Jody, 'it started like this. Hamish's mum and dad are always fussing over him, and trying to make sure he doesn't catch a cold and all that sort of thing. They decided that school lunch wasn't good for him so they insisted that he bring a packed lunch. At first Mrs Chipchase was furious and tried to stop him eating it. But then –'

'Quiet over there!' snapped Mrs Chipchase. 'This is your last warning.

Teachers, indeed,' she muttered to herself. Then she turned to Hamish Bigmore, and a sickly smile crossed her face. 'And how's my favourite friend today, eh?'

'Very well, thank you, Mrs Chipchase,' cooed Hamish. 'And look what mummy has given me today, Mrs Chipchase.' Hamish pointed to the packed lunch he had spread out on the table in front of him.

'Yum, yum,' said Mrs Chipchase, licking her lips. 'What do I see there?'

'Sandwiches of home-cured ham,' said Hamish Bigmore, 'with your favourite tomato and gherkin relish.'

'Yum, yum,' said Mrs Chipchase. 'And what else has my favourite friend brought with him?'

'A salad of wild mushrooms, garden lettuce and grated carrot, and

a large pot of mummy's home-made yoghurt flavoured with the very best honey.'

'Yum, yum, yum,' said Mrs Chipchase. 'Well, my favourite friend, you won't be wanting all of that, will you?'

'No, Mrs Chipchase,' answered Hamish Bigmore. 'In fact, I won't be wanting any of it. I don't feel very well. Do take it away.'

'Oh, may I?' said Mrs Chipchase, who was almost dribbling at the mouth. 'Oh, aren't you just my favourite friend?' And she scooped up Hamish's packed lunch, every bit of it, and made for the kitchen door. 'I'll be back in a minute, my favourite friend!'

'The same thing happens every day,' Jody explained to Mr Majeika. 'Every day he brings a delicious packed lunch, and every day he pretends he's ill and gives it all to Mrs Chipchase.'

'But why?' asked Mr Majeika. 'Doesn't he want to eat it?'

Thomas shook his head. 'Hamish Bigmore wouldn't want to eat nice food like that. There's only one thing that Hamish likes. Ssh! Here she comes again.'

Mrs Chipchase was coming out of

the kitchen. 'I'm so sorry my favourite friend is feeling poorly,' she cooed. 'I've brought him a little something from Cook and me to make him feel better. Only he mustn't go giving any of it to the other children, because he knows they aren't allowed to have any. There you are, my favourite friend.' And she handed Hamish Bigmore a huge bar of chocolate.

'Every day?' asked Mr Majeika, when school dinner was over and they were out in the playground.

'Every day,' sighed Jody. 'Every day he brings a yummy packed lunch, and every day Mrs Chipchase carts it off to the kitchen, and she and Cook eat every scrap of it themselves. And every day, as a reward, she gives Hamish an enormous bar of chocolate.'

'Dear, dear,' said Mr Majeika. 'This can't go on.'

'That's what we've been saying for ages,' said Thomas. 'But we don't know how to stop it.'

'We don't want to talk to Mr Potter about it,' explained Jody, 'because that would be telling tales, and anyway, Mr Potter is just as frightened of Mrs Chipchase as we are.'

'There just doesn't seem to be anything we can do about it,' sighed Pete.

Mr Majeika thought for a moment. 'Oh, yes, there is,' he said.

At dinner time the next day, Hamish Bigmore spread his packed lunch on the table as usual.

'And what has my favourite friend got for me today?' cooed Mrs Chipchase.

'Italian salami on rye bread,' said Hamish Bigmore. 'A seafood cocktail dressed with pink mayonnaise, and home-baked sesame seed rolls.'

'Yum, yum, yum,' said Mrs Chipchase. 'All my favourites.'

'Then there's chocolate dessert made

with fresh cream, and a French goat's milk cheese that mum and dad brought back from a weekend in Paris,.'

Mrs Chipchase rolled her eyes. 'Cook and I are just going to love that,' she said. 'I mean – is there anything you won't be wanting, my favourite friend?'

'Just take the lot, Mrs Chipchase,' said Hamish impatiently, 'and bring me my chocolate.'

Her eyes popping with greed, Mrs Chipchase stuffed all Hamish's food back into the bag in which Hamish had brought it, and headed for the kitchen door.

Suddenly she crashed right into Mr Majeika, who was coming out of the kitchen. The packed lunch went flying.

'Oh I am so sorry,' said Mr Majeika.

'I was just saying how do you do to Cook, as we'd never met before. Here, let me pick everything up for you.' He put the packed lunch together again, waving his hands over it in rather a peculiar fashion.

'Teachers!' snorted Mrs Chipchase, when Mr Majeika handed the packed lunch back to her. 'Teachers!' she snorted again, and banged the kitchen door behind her.

Hamish Bigmore sat waiting for his chocolate. 'What are *you* doing here?' he said suspiciously to Mr Majeika.

'Oh, I've just come to watch everyone eat their lunch,' said Mr Majeika cheerfully. 'All their different kinds of lunch.'

At that moment there was a loud scream from the kitchen. Two screams, in fact: Cook and Mrs Chipchase.

'Dear me,' said Mr Majeika. 'Something seems to be a little wrong. Shall we go and see?'

In the kitchen Cook and Mrs Chipchase were dancing about on top of the table, as if something was trying to eat them.

'Help!' they were screaming. 'Help! Take them away!'

The floor was covered with wriggling creatures. There were worms, snails, slugs, cockroaches, enormous spiders and some very peculiar-looking creepy-crawlies.

'Help! Help!' screamed Cook and Mrs Chipchase.

'What are they?' Jody asked Mr

Majeika. 'Where did they all come from?'

'Those,' said Mr Majeika, pointing at the creepy-crawlies, the worms, snails, slugs, spiders and cockroaches, 'were in Hamish Bigmore's packed lunch today.'

'Where's my chocolate?' said a cross voice. It was Hamish Bigmore. 'Mrs Chipchase, your favourite friend wants his chocolate.'

'Favourite friend, indeed!' screamed out Mrs Chipchase, purple in the face. 'How dare you treat Cook and me like that! What a horrid trick, to put all those creepy things in our packed lunch.'

'But – but it wasn't me, Mrs Chipchase,' spluttered Hamish. 'Really, it wasn't!'

'Well, if it wasn't you,' shouted Mrs Chipchase, 'then it must have been the other horrid brats. What a way to treat Cook and me after all the years of service we've given the school. I shall tell Mr Potter that we're leaving right away, and we won't be back! Oh, won't he let you have it when he hears about this!'

'That worked even better than you planned, didn't it, Mr Majeika?' asked Jody late that afternoon. Mrs Chipchase and Cook had stormed off, and everyone was feeling very jolly – except Hamish Bigmore, who was sulking in a corner.

'Yes, it did rather,' said Mr Majeika. 'I never guessed she'd walk out. I just thought she'd be cross with Hamish.'

'How did you do it?' asked Thomas. 'Did you magic the packed lunch so that it was full of all those creatures?'

Mr Majeika nodded. 'I thought it was time that Cook and Mrs Chipchase sampled the sort of thing that wizards eat for their lunch. Actually, they taste very nice – though I suppose they wouldn't be everyone's favourite dish.' He sighed. 'That was easy enough to do. But I'm going to need some strong magic to help me now.'

'What do you mean?' asked Pete.

'I've told Mr Potter I'll cook the school dinners for a week until a new cook has been found,' said Mr Majeika.

'Hurray!' exclaimed Jody. 'Good food at last!'

Mr Majeika shook his head. 'I wouldn't be too certain about that. The only sort of food I know how to cook is the kind that wizards eat. I've really no idea how to make the sort of thing that children like.'

'It should be easy,' said Thomas. 'There's a menu pinned up on the school notice-board. It tells you what's going to be served for lunch. You just cook the food it says for each day. And I expect you could find a book to tell you how to do the actual cooking.'

'Maybe,' said Mr Majeika rather doubtfully. 'Anyway, I shall have a helper. I've told Hamish Bigmore to be my potato-peeler and washer-up. I thought the hard work would do him good.'

Hamish Bigmore glared at them from his corner.

For four days, from Monday to Thursday, they had marvellous food. Mr Majeika produced delicious fish

fingers, beefburgers, baked beans,
chips, ice-cream and all the other
things that everyone really liked. 'It's
quite easy,' he said. 'You just buy the
things from the shops and read the
instructions on the packets.' He kept
Hamish hard at work, pushing the
trolley, collecting the empty plates
and washing up. Hamish looked
furious, but there was nothing he
could do about it.

Then came Friday, Mr Majeika's last

day as school cook – Mr Potter had announced that somebody new was coming on Monday. 'I wonder what Mr Majeika's made for us today,' said Jody. 'I forgot to look at the menu.'

'I bet it's marvellous, whatever it is,' said Thomas. 'No more bony sausages, no more greasy old spaghetti. Ah, here comes Hamish with it now.'

Hamish was pushing the dinner-trolley out of the kitchen. It was piled high with covered dishes.

'What is it today, Hamish?' Peter called out.

'You'll see,' said Hamish, grinning his usual nasty grin.

'I don't know what you've got to smile about, Hamish,' said Thomas. 'No chocolate for you any more.'

Hamish didn't reply, but went

round the tables handing out the dishes. Mr Majeika came out of the kitchen wearing an apron. 'I do hope it's all right,' he said anxiously. 'It seems rather an odd thing to give to schoolchildren, though wizards would certainly like it.'

'What is it, Mr Majeika?' asked Jody.

'Well,' said Mr Majeika, 'you'd better take off the lid and see.'

The children lifted the lids off their plates. They stared at what was on the plates. And beady eyes stared back at them.

'Toads!' shrieked Jody. 'Toads sitting in piles of moss and stones! Is this a joke, Mr Majeika?'

Mr Majeika shook his head sadly. 'Not at all. Haven't I got it right? Toad-in-the-hole did seem a funny thing to have on the menu, but Hamish Bigmore said you often ate it.'

'Yes,' said Peter, 'we do, but it's not supposed to be quite like this, Mr Majeika. Oh dear, it seems that Hamish has had the last word as usual!'

2. *Three Little Pigs*

'Pigs!' snorted Hamish Bigmore. 'Horses! Sheep! Cows! What a silly babyish waste of time.'

Mr Potter was pinning up a notice on the school board:

VISIT TO THE BARTYSHIRE
FARM PARK
to see rare breeds of pigs, horses, sheep, cattle and other animals.
Don't be late!
Bus leaves Monday at 9 a.m. sharp.

'How stupid can you get,' muttered Hamish. 'Why don't we go and see something useful, like a gun museum or a computer factory? Rare breeds! I never heard such silly nonsense.'

'I should think they might have a

job for you at the Farm Park,' said
Thomas. 'They could put you in a field
labelled "Rarest breed of all. Hamish
Bigmore – the only one ever
discovered. Thank goodness!"'

Hamish kicked him hard on the
ankle.

'It's very annoying,' said Mr Potter.
'I've never known them send too

small a bus before. I can't think what we're going to do.'

It was Monday morning and very cold, and a bus that seated only twenty-nine people was standing outside the gates of St Barty's School. There were thirty children in Class Three, plus Mr Majeika and Mr Potter, who was coming on the expedition as well, making thirty-two in all.

'Couldn't three of the children sit on the floor?' asked Mr Majeika.

Mr Potter shook his head. 'The driver won't allow it. He says he's only permitted to carry twenty-nine, and he'll get in trouble with the police if he crams any more in.'

'Well,' said Mr Majeika, 'maybe you could take the expedition to the Farm Park by yourself, and I could stay behind and look after the two children who can't go on the bus.'

The truth was that Mr Majeika didn't want to go to the Farm Park any more than Hamish Bigmore did. It was a very cold day for being outdoors.

Mr Potter shook his head. 'No, I don't think so, Mr Majeika. If you haven't been to the Farm Park yourself, how could you organize a project about the rare breeds?'

Mr Majeika sighed. Organizing projects and all that sort of thing still seemed very odd to him. He wished, not for the first time, that teaching was as easy as being a wizard, when all you had to do was make spells and enjoy yourself.

'Very well, Mr Potter,' he said sadly. 'If I take two children with me, I expect we can catch an ordinary bus at the bus-stop. We'll soon get there. Now,' and he turned to Class Three, 'who would like to come with me on an ordinary bus?'

Everyone put up their hands except Hamish Bigmore. There was so much argument about who was going to have the fun of going with Mr Majeika that in the end they had to put everyone's names in a hat. Mr Majeika shook them all up and picked out two.

The names chosen were Thomas and Jody.

Peter was very upset. 'I'm going to have an awful boring journey by myself,' he said, 'while you two are having a lovely time with Mr Majeika. It isn't fair!'

Mr Majeika, Thomas and Jody had to wait a long time before a bus came, and they had a long slow journey. On the way they even had to change buses.

As they got nearer to the Farm Park, it started to get foggy. 'What does this remind you of?' asked Mr Majeika.

'The journey we made to the haunted hotel,' Jody said at once. 'But that was in a really creepy place up on the hills, and this is just ordinary countryside. You wouldn't expect to

find Wilhelmina Worlock in a place like this!'

'I was just thinking,' said Thomas, 'that it's a long time – thank goodness! – since we've seen anything of Miss Worlock. Maybe she's decided to leave us alone at last.'

Wilhelmina Worlock was a witch, and a very nasty witch at that. She had arrived at St Barty's and tried to turn Class Three into the Wilhelmina

Worlock School of Music. Hamish Bigmore had liked her because she called him her Star Pupil, but everyone else hated her because she made their fingers itch if they didn't practise their musical instruments. Mr Majeika had had to wage a battle against her, with each of them turning into different animals, before he could get rid of her. And soon afterwards she lured them to a haunted hotel and tried to frighten them in revenge. That time, Mr Majeika had managed to take her off to Ancient Rome, where he and Class Three had left her about to be eaten by lions.

'I expect that's the last we'll ever see of her,' said Jody.

'I hope so,' said Mr Majeika.

It was nearly lunch-time when they

finally reached the Farm Park, and the
fog had become very thick. 'It doesn't
look very nice here,' said Jody.

It certainly didn't. The Farm Park
was just a big field, down a lane from
a road that seemed to lead nowhere.
There was a brick building labelled
'Café, Light Refreshments,' and a

wooden hut where someone was supposed to sit and take people's money. And beyond that, Mr Majeika, Thomas and Jody could hear snuffles and snorts and grunts from the animals.

The odd thing was, there were no people anywhere. The fog was so thick that it was hard to see very far, but there was certainly no one in the wooden hut to take their money, so they walked straight in. When they got inside, they couldn't see any sign of the rest of Class Three.

'Perhaps they haven't got here yet,' suggested Thomas.

'Oh, but they must have,' said Mr Majeika. 'They started a long time before us, and their bus came straight here. I saw it parked outside in the road and it was empty.'

'Well,' said Jody, 'we'd better have a look round. But it seems pretty creepy to me.'

It *was* creepy. The fog swirled around, and the animals stared sadly at them through the fences. They didn't look happy. They seemed to have been given plenty to eat, and there was lots of lush green grass for the horses and sheep and cattle to chew, but something seemed to be wrong. They all had the oddest expressions on their faces.

'They're not like any animals I've ever seen,' said Jody. 'I mean, I know they're rare breeds, but even so, they're very strange. I mean, look at that horse!'

A horse was staring intently at them across the fence. A notice said:

HORSUS BANKUS MANAGERIUS
A speesies very often found in
British towns
Can be very narsty if asked for money

'How very peculiar,' said Mr Majeika.
'Horsus Bankus Managerius? What
can that mean?'

'It's Latin,' said Thomas. 'Horsus
means horse.'

'No, it doesn't,' said Jody. 'We

learnt some Latin last year with Mr
Potter, when we did a project on the
Ancient Romans, and I remember the
word for horse. It's *equus*. People
often use Latin names for different
types of animals or flowers, but this
has been written by someone who
doesn't know Latin.'

'And doesn't know how to spell
either,' said Thomas. 'Speesies and
narsty aren't right.'

'What does Bankus Managerius
mean?' asked Mr Majeika, very
puzzled.

'That's obvious,' said Thomas. 'It's
Bank Manager. My dad is always
complaining about his bank manager,
because he won't lend him any more
money. Come to think of it, the horse
does look a bit like a bank manager.'

'I'm sure he's listening to you,' said

Jody. 'And look, he's nodding! Oh, let's go, I don't like this at all.'

'It's certainly most peculiar,' said Mr Majeika. 'Let's go and see the pigs. I'm sure they'll be more cheerful.'

On the way to the pigs they passed some other creatures with curious names. There was a Goatus Trafficus Wardenus, which was black with yellow stripes, a Sheepus Rudus

Policemanus, which had a sort of bump on its head that looked rather like a helmet, and a Bullus Sillius Headmasterus, a very dazed-looking bull that was trying to scratch its head with its hoof.

'It's very funny,' said Jody, 'but that bull has something about it that reminds me of Mr Potter. Oh look, here are the pigs.'

The pigs were making a lot more noise than the other animals, but they didn't seem to be any happier. Three of the smaller ones rushed up to the fence and began to squeal at Thomas, Jody and Mr Majeika.

'Poor little things,' said Jody. 'I wonder what can be wrong with them.'

Thomas bent down to pat them and then stood up looking rather white in

the face. 'I can't believe it,' he said,
'but do you know who that pig
reminds me of?' He pointed at a piglet
that was bouncing up and down even
more than the others.

Jody looked at it carefully. 'Your
brother Peter,' she said. As if in
answer, the piglet squealed wildly.

'And the one next to it is crying,'
said Thomas, 'just like Melanie always

does in class.'

'And the third one,' said Jody, 'looks just like Pandora Green. Are we imagining it, Mr Majeika, or is something very, very peculiar going on?'

Mr Majeika was looking worried. 'I think we'd better go and find the owner of this place,' he said. 'We must ask for an explanation.'

They made their way back towards the main gate. When they got to the wooden hut, they saw that the gate itself had been closed. It was fastened with a big chain and padlock and there was barbed wire across the top of it.

'We've been locked in!' said Jody nervously. 'There must be some human person around to have done that.'

'Yes, there is,' whispered Thomas. 'There's someone in the ticket office now.'

'Come to buy your tickets, have you, dearies?' hissed a voice. 'Come to Wilhelmina's Farm Park, have you? Well, isn't that nice! Come and join the family!'

'Wilhelmina Worlock!' said Mr Majeika. 'I might have guessed that you were behind all this.'

Miss Worlock took them on a tour of her Farm Park. 'Been building this up all year, I has,' she explained. 'Ever since I got back from Ancient Rome. Wilhelmina thought she'd have a bit of fun, dearies, and not just with schoolchildren this time. She's been getting her own back on everyone who's been nasty to her.'

'Bank managers and traffic wardens and policemen?' said Thomas.

'That's right, dearie. Very fine animals, they is, and now they won't trouble poor Wilhelmina any more. And now, dearies, it's your turn. You two kids'll make very fine piglets like the rest, though as for *you* –' and she turned to Mr Majeika, 'we'll need to make something special out of you, my fine wizard. I should think a worm would suit you nicely. Yes, we'll turn you into a wriggly worm, and then these little pigs can gobble you up.'

'Can't you do something, Mr Majeika?' said Jody breathlessly. 'Can't you cast a spell before she does?'

Mr Majeika sighed heavily. 'Yes, Jody, I can. But we've been through all that before. When Wilhemina and I have a battle of magic, it's anybody's guess who's going to win. Really, Wilhelmina,' he turned to Miss Worlock, 'aren't you getting a bit old for this sort of thing? Isn't it time you taught your evil arts to someone a bit younger – perhaps to Hamish Bigmore?'

'Yes, where is Hamish Bigmore?' asked Thomas. 'What did you turn him into? A piggier pig than all the rest?'

Miss Worlock shook her head. 'Your friend Wizard Majeika has guessed right,' she said. 'Don't forget that darling little Hamish has always been my Star Pupil. I'm teaching him to take over all Wilhelmina's clever witchery. Right now he's sitting over there in the café, studying my books of spells very, very hard. Oh, he's going to be a clever little wizard, is our Hamish.'

'H'mm, maybe,' said Mr Majeika thoughtfully. 'But when I peeped through the café window just now, your Star Pupil wasn't working hard at all, Wilhelmina. At least, he wasn't working on your spell books. He was working his hardest to eat up all the chocolate and sweets in the place.'

'What!' screamed Wilhelmina. 'The

greedy little brat! I'll turn him into a toad, the ungrateful blighter. Just wait!' And, muttering to herself, she bustled off towards the café.

'Quick!' whispered Mr Majeika. 'Let's look in here!' And he dived into the ticket hut, emerging a moment later with an old leather-bound notebook. 'Yes, here it is!' he said excitedly. 'This is the spell Wilhelmina

used this morning to turn Class Three into animals. Quick now, and I'll reverse it.'

He muttered some words to himself and waved his arms. The air seemed to quiver in front of Jody and Thomas. A moment later they could hear cheering.

'Look!' said Jody. 'The fog has cleared, and there's Peter and Melanie and Pandora climbing over the fence. They're not pigs any more!'

'All of Class Three are here,' said Thomas. 'There's Mr Potter in that field. He's managed to scratch his head at last – he couldn't do it when he had hoofs instead of hands.'

'And look at all those other people,' said Mr Majeika. 'The bank manager and the traffic warden and the policeman, and lots more – all the people who've annoyed Wilhelmina. They look awfully pleased to have got their real shapes back.'

'But what about Wilhelmina?' said Jody. 'Won't she turn them all back again, and us too?'

'I nearly forgot!' said Mr Majeika, snatching up the book of spells again just as Wilhelmina emerged from the café, clutching Hamish Bigmore by his ear.

'Quite right, Wizard Majeika,' she snarled. 'My Star Pupil wasn't being a Star Pupil at all. He's just eaten Wilhelmina's entire stock of chocolate drops. Nasty little brat!' And she tweaked Hamish's ear. 'Well, I see you've been having fun in my absence, Wizard Majeika. Mucking about with Auntie Wilhelmina's animals, eh?'

'Yes, Wilhelmina,' said Mr Majeika,
'I have. And since I've spoilt your
Farm Park, maybe you ought to have
one very special animal that you can
keep. I'm talking about *you*,
Wilhelmina.' And before Miss
Worlock could stop him, he had
mumbled a spell out of her book and
waved his arms at her.

There was a puff of smoke and
Wilhelmina vanished. On the ground
where she had been standing was a
fish tank. And inside the fish tank,
swimming angrily around, was a large
goldfish.

Mr Majeika picked up the fish tank
and handed it to the bank manager.
'You might like to look after it in your
bank,' he said. 'And then later you
can pass it on to the traffic warden and
the policeman. It might be kind to let

her go in a few months, but
meanwhile you might as well give her
the treatment she gave you.'
Miss Worlock had changed the bus
driver into an animal too (labelled
Donkeyus Busus Driverus), and he
was so pleased to have been changed
back by Mr Majeika that he let all of
Class Three, and Mr Majeika and Mr
Potter, ride home in the bus, even

though some of them had to sit on the floor.

'What I don't understand,' said Jody to Mr Majeika, 'is how you knew that Hamish was eating chocolate instead of studying spells. You didn't even see him.'

'It was only a guess,' said Mr Majeika. 'But if you let Hamish loose in a place that's full of chocolate, there's going to be only one thing on his mind.'

Hamish glared at them. 'If you'd arrived five minutes later,' he said, 'I'd have learnt some really clever spells, and then you'd have been in real trouble.'

'And what was it like as a pig?' Thomas asked Pete.

'Not bad,' said Pete. 'But we were so hungry we ate everything she gave us, even though it was just kitchen scraps – potato peelings, rotten apples and that sort of thing. And, do you know, it tasted much better than school dinners.'

'I can't believe that,' said Thomas.

3. *The Ghost Hunter*

'Now, everyone,' said Mr Potter at Assembly, 'it's the School Fête on Saturday, and I want you all to behave yourselves. Lady Debenham, the head of the school governors, is coming to open it, and she's a thoroughly fussy person. I mean –' he corrected himself hastily, 'she gets very upset if children behave badly, and quite right too.'

'You know Lady Debenham,' whispered Pete to Jody. 'She's the silly old bag who lives in the big house at the top of the road.'

'She's got a face like a bent bicycle-wheel,' whispered Thomas, 'and a temper to match. She's always telling us off for running home from school and for shouting in the street. She wants us to behave like stuffed dolls.'

'I'm afraid,' continued Mr Potter from the platform, 'that Lady Debenham is particularly cross with this school at the moment. It seems that some of you have been pulling up the flowers in her garden, and she's very angry about it. Someone even painted

on one of her trees, which made her furious. In fact, she's talking about closing St Barty's down and sending you all to St James's School instead.'

There was a groan from everyone. St James's was a posh school a short distance down the road. It was half empty, because no one wanted to be sent there. No one except Hamish Bigmore.

'I wish Lady Windbag *would* close rotten St Barty's,' muttered Hamish to Thomas, Pete and Jody as they crossed the playground on the way to Class Three. 'Then we wouldn't have to be taught by stupid Mr Majeika.'

'I bet it was you who picked Lady Debenham's flowers and painted on the tree,' said Jody.

'Of course it was,' replied Hamish, grinning widely.

'Well, if you're so keen to go to stupid St James's,' said Thomas, 'why don't you tell your parents to take you away from St Barty's and send you there? They always do everything you want.'

Hamish scowled. 'I keep on asking

them. But my mother thinks Mr Majeika is *sweet*. I ask you! She says that none of the teachers at St James's would be as kind to me. Huh!'

'She may be right,' said Jody. 'By the way, Hamish, why are you limping?'

Hamish scowled again. 'That old cow Lady Debenham has put barbed wire round her garden, and I scratched myself getting in. But I got my own back. I pulled up all her rubbishy daffodils! I'll do anything to close down this rotten old school.'

'This morning,' said Mr Majeika to Class Three, 'we're going to get on with our project.'

'Not wild flowers and plants again?' groaned Hamish Bigmore.

'That's right,' said Mr Majeika.

'Why can't we do something sensible,' grumbled Hamish, 'like space weapons, or the history of torture?'

'Come along now, Hamish,' said Mr Majeika patiently, 'there's lots of work to do this morning. I want you all to make drawings of herbs I've brought in, and write notes on the things they were used for in the old days.'

'What sort of things, Mr Majeika?' asked Thomas.

'Well,' said Mr Majeika, 'before people got pills and medicines from the chemist's, like they do today, they made mixtures of herbs when people were ill. They gathered plants like lavender and mint from the fields and hedges. They believed these plants could cure things if they were mixed together in the right quantities. And it seems to have worked.'

'I've never heard such rubbish,'
growled Hamish. 'You can't cure
people with plants! You need X-rays
and operations and blood transfusions
and antibiotics and things like that.
When I grow up, I'm going to be a
famous brain surgeon.'

Mr Majeika smiled. 'Well, Hamish,
you'd be surprised at what herbs
could cure. In fact, they still can. Am I
right in thinking that you've got a bit

of a scratch on your knee?'

Hamish glared at him. 'What if I have?'

'Hmm, yes,' said Mr Majeika, coming to look at it. 'A nasty scratch. It looks as if it might have been made by barbed wire . . . Well, Hamish, I've got an old book of herbal remedies here, so let's see what we can do for you.'

Hamish complained, but in no time at all Mr Majeika had looked up some instructions in his book, and he got the rest of Class Three to mix up herbs that they had been gathering on country walks during the term. Mr Majeika showed them how to make the herbs into a sort of paste. Then he smeared the paste on Hamish's knee and stood back to see what would happen.

What happened was that Hamish
Bigmore vanished. Where he had
been sitting, there was an empty
chair.

'Oh dear!' cried Mr Majeika. 'I must
have got the wrong remedy.'

'Has he turned into a frog again?'
asked Jody, remembering what had
happened when Mr Majeika first came
to teach Class Three.

'No, I haven't,' said Hamish's voice.

'I'm over here.' They all turned round, but they couldn't see him.

'Where?' said Pete.

'Here,' said Hamish's voice. And the waste-paper basket rose from the floor, floated across the room in mid-air and emptied itself carefully over Peter's head.

'Oh dear,' said Mr Majeika, examining his book of herbal remedies. 'Two pages have stuck together. What starts as a recipe for curing cuts and scratches turns into a spell for making people invisible.'

Having an invisible Hamish ought to have been pleasant. 'After all,' said Thomas, 'he's an ugly brute, and it's nice not to be able to see him.' But it was really very tiresome.

Mr Majeika searched desperately

through his notebooks to find a spell that would make Hamish visible again, but in the meantime Hamish was having fun. No one was allowed a moment's peace.

Anything wet, like paints or ink, kept floating off the shelves and into people's faces, or were smeared all over their clothes. And when anyone tried to sit down their chair was pulled away, so that they fell on to the floor.

When Hamish got bored with tricks like that, he went around pulling people's hair and pinching them.

Everyone kept trying to catch him, but it was no use. Thomas and Jody managed to get hold of his jersey, though of course they couldn't see it, and Peter was trying to tie him to a chair with his own belt when Hamish bit him very hard on the ear. Peter yelled and lost his grip, and Hamish wriggled free, upsetting chairs and tables all across the room. After a while they just gave up trying to stop him, hoping that Mr Majeika would soon find the right spell. The invisible Hamish now occupied himself by pulling out everyone's drawers where they kept their workbooks and things they had brought to school, and then making a great big untidy pile of everything in the middle of the room.

At last Mr Majeika called out, 'I think I've got it! It's another herbal remedy.'

They helped him mix up the herbs as quickly as they could, though of course Hamish kept getting in the way. At last they'd made up a new paste, and after chasing the invisible Hamish round the room, Thomas, Jody and Peter managed to catch him again, and Mr Majeika smeared some of the herb paste over him.

Suddenly they could see Hamish again. He was grinning all over his face; obviously he'd been having the time of his life.

'Well, well,' said Mr Majeika, 'that should teach me not to meddle with things I don't understand properly. These herbal remedies are much stronger than you'd expect. Now, Hamish, as the first part of your punishment for such terrible behaviour, you can clear up all the mess you've made.'

When Thomas and Pete got to school the next morning, they found Mr Majeika looking very tired and gloomy. 'What's the matter?' they asked.

'The herbal pastes have disappeared,' he explained.

'The paste that made Hamish invisible?' asked Thomas.

'Yes,' said Mr Majeika, 'and the one that made him visible again. I kept Hamish here for hours after school, making him clear up the mess, and it was only after he'd gone that I remembered I hadn't put away those pastes, or thrown them away, which would have been the sensible thing to do. If it gets into the wrong hands, that invisibility mixture could do awful harm.'

'Well,' said Pete, 'it's probably in Hamish Bigmore's hands, or at least his pocket, and I can't think of anything more awful than that.'

When Mr Majeika asked him, Hamish said he didn't know what had happened to the herbal pastes. But he was grinning wickedly. Mr Majeika made him turn out his pockets, but there was no sign of the invisibility mixture.

'He's probably hidden it at home,' said Jody. 'Anyway, I'm sure we'll soon know about it if he has got it.'

But Hamish didn't become invisible

again that day, or the next, or the day after that. He was as badly behaved as usual, but everyone could see him all the time. So, after a while, Mr Majeika decided that the pastes must have been thrown away by the school cleaner. 'That's a relief,' he said, 'especially with the School Fête tomorrow. We'd have been in real trouble if Hamish had managed to make himself invisible during the Fête.'

'Ah, here she comes,' said Mr Potter, who had been waiting at the school gate in his best suit with a flower in the buttonhole, looking anxiously at his watch. He bustled up to meet a very grand-looking woman in a hat.

'Couldn't help being late, Potter,' snapped Lady Debenham. 'Had to go

to a meeting of the Society for
Psychical Investigation.'

'Bicycles, your ladyship?' asked Mr
Potter vaguely. 'I didn't know you
rode one.'

'No, no, man,' snapped Lady
Debenham. '*Psychical*. It means
ghosts. The society wants to prove
that there really are ghosts, so we go

around looking for them.'

'Ah, yes,' said Mr Potter unsurely. He led Lady Debenham to a small platform that had been set up in the school playground. When she had taken her seat, Mr Potter made a short welcome speech.

Everyone clapped, and Lady Debenham got to her feet and came to the microphone. 'Thank you, Potter,' she snapped. 'Now, children, behave yourselves, or I shall have to think seriously about closing down St Barty's and sending you all to St James's. Remember that! And now I declare this Fête well and truly open.'

Everyone clapped again, and Jody came up to the platform carrying a big bunch of flowers, beautifully wrapped. She had been chosen to present them to Lady Debenham.

Lady Debenham smiled rather frostily. She was just about to take the flowers from Jody when they flew out of Jody's hands, rose in the air and squashed themselves against Lady Debenham's face.

'Oh no!' said Thomas to Pete. 'I'd just been wondering why we hadn't seen Hamish Bigmore this afternoon, and now I know.'

'He must have got that invisibility paste, just as Mr Majeika suspected,' said Pete. 'Now we're really in for it!'

Lady Debenham was very, very angry. Her elegant make-up had been smudged by the stalks of the flowers, and her glasses knocked off. At first she blamed Jody, but fortunately Mr Potter had seen what had happened. 'It must have been a sudden strong gust of wind, your ladyship,' he said soothingly to Lady Debenham.

After a few minutes Lady Debenham had calmed down a bit, and she began to go round the stalls with Mr Potter.

Her first call was at the Lucky Dip. She was just bending down to reach into the tub of sawdust when her legs flew into the air and she landed face-first in the tub.

'Hamish again!' said Jody to
Thomas and Pete. 'This is awful.'

It took some time for Lady
Debenham to get the sawdust out of
her hair and clothes. By now she was
in a furious temper. Mr Potter was
trying to persuade her that she had
slipped on a patch of mud, but she
didn't believe him. 'Somebody is
playing a trick on me,' she snapped.

'Well, you know what I said I'd do if your children were naughty, don't you, Potter?'

'Yes, your ladyship,' muttered Mr Potter gloomily, wondering if the head teacher of St James's would give him a job when St Barty's was closed down. Then he cheered up a bit. 'I tell you what, your ladyship, why not come and sample one of Class Two's delicious home-made ice-creams?'

Lady Debenham was still very cross, but she agreed. 'Oh no,' whispered Jody, as she and Thomas and Pete followed Lady Debenham and Mr Potter across the playground. 'I can guess what's going to happen now. We must do something to stop Hamish!'

'I've got an idea,' said Pete. 'There's a sack race going on over there. Let's get a sack and try to catch Hamish in it before he does any more harm.'

Snatching a sack, they headed for the ice-cream stall. Already a large vanilla ice was hovering in the air over Lady Debenham's head. The invisible Hamish must have climbed on to the stall. 'He's going to smother it all over her!' said Jody. 'Quick! Jump!'

They jumped and brought the sack

down over what felt like Hamish Bigmore. Unfortunately, they brought it down over Lady Debenham as well.

'It's all right,' said Mr Majeika, bustling up with two jars in his hands. 'I've found the invisibility paste and the one to make you visible again, both of them in Hamish's drawer. He must have put them there this afternoon after making himself invisible. Now we can put a stop to his pranks.'

'Too late,' said Jody, pointing at the ground where a pair of legs were sticking out of the sack, kicking wildly. 'It's Lady Debenham in that sack. And I'm afraid this is the end of St Barty's.'

From the sack came muffled shouts. Lady Debenham was fighting the invisible Hamish Bigmore.

Mr Majeika, Jody, Thomas and Pete
got the sack off her and, while Mr
Majeika grabbed hold of Hamish and
smeared him with the paste to make
him visible again, the others tried to
brush her down and calm her. But to
their amazement, she was smiling.

'We're so sorry, Lady Debenham,'
they said to her.

'Sorry?' beamed Lady Debenham.

'It was the greatest moment of my life. A real ghost! I couldn't see it, but I could hear it and feel it. My society will be delighted. And as for St Barty's, far from closing it down, I'm very, very proud of it. It's the only school in England with its own ghost!'

Jody, Thomas and Pete looked at each other, and at Mr Majeika and Hamish.

'Hamish Bigmore isn't going to like this one little bit,' Jody said, grinning. 'But he's saved St Barty's!'